The
Race

Written by Jan Swanberg
Illustrated by Ron Lipking

Hooked On Phonics®

The cars are all set
to get in the race.

All of them want
to be in first place.

Quick! Get the pump!

Quick! Shut the hatch!

Quick! Drop the top!

Quick! Fix the latch!

Now check the tires
with a big kick.

Now check the gas,
and make it quick!

BANG! It's the gun.
The race will begin!

The van wants to go!
They all want to win!

The hot rod goes HUM!
The big truck is hot.

The rocket gets set.
The red van cannot.

The hot rod spins.
The big truck slips.

The red van skids.
The rocket zips.

Oh, no! Look at that!
The track is too slick!

The track is too wet!
Do not hit that brick!

Oh, no! Oh, my my!
The big truck is stuck!

It's stuck in the mud!
Oh, no! What bad luck!

The hot rod is quick.
Then a big tire pops!

The rocket's on track.
But the red van stops!

CLING CLANG! Neck and neck!
The cars all go THUMP!

ZIP ZAP! What a race!
The van hits a bump!

BANG! It's a crash!
The rocket goes THUD!

Look out for the ditch!
Look out for the mud!

The pig drops the flag.
The rocket car grins.
The ribbon is his!
The rocket car wins!